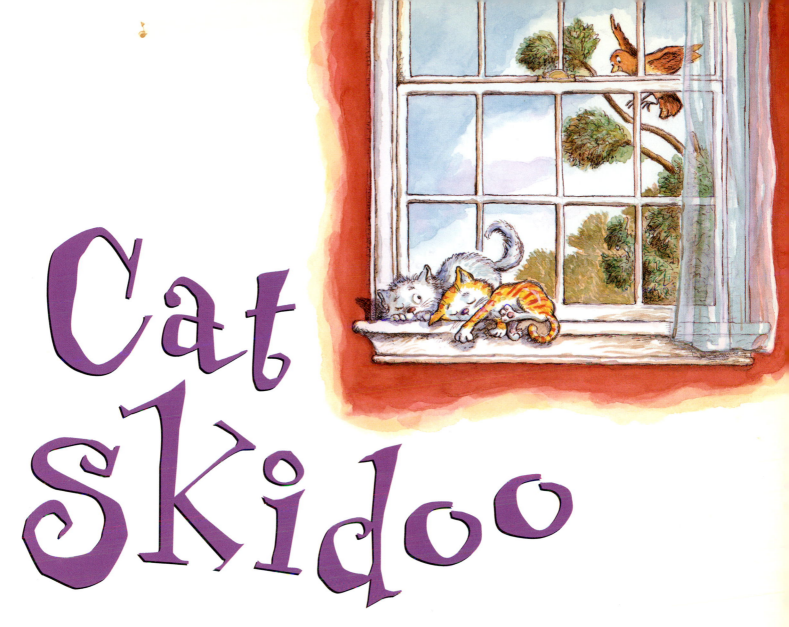

Cat Skidoo

by Bethany Roberts
illustrated by R. W. Alley

Henry Holt and Company
New York

To Shasta, Sachi, and Shinook—skidoo cats all!
—B. R.

For Naomi and Joan, always skidooing!
—R. W. A.

Henry Holt and Company, LLC
Publishers since 1866
115 West 18th Street
New York, New York 10011
www.henryholt.com

Henry Holt is a registered trademark of Henry Holt and Company, LLC
Text copyright © 2004 by Barbara Beverage
Illustrations copyright © 2004 by R. W. Alley
All rights reserved.
Distributed in Canada by H. B. Fenn and Company Ltd.

Library of Congress Cataloging-in-Publication Data
Roberts, Bethany.
Cat Skidoo / by Bethany Roberts; illustrated by R. W. Alley.
Summary: Two active kittens romp outdoors before going back inside for a nap.
[1. Cats—Fiction. 2. Stories in rhyme.] I. Alley, R. W. (Robert W.), ill. II. Title.
PZ8.3.R5295Cat 2004 [E]—dc22 2003012249

ISBN 0-8050-6710-8 / First Edition—2004 / Designed by Patrick Collins
The artist used pen and ink and watercolors on Strathmore paper to create the illustrations for this book.
Printed in the United States of America on acid-free paper. ∞

10 9 8 7 6 5 4 3 2 1

Kittens in the window—
one cat, two,

jumping down for . . .

CAT SKIDOO!

Pit-pat,
    pit-pat,
across the floor.
Mew!
    Mew!
Out the door!

Kittens in the garden—
one cat, two,

sniffing,
digging,

CAT SKIDOO!

Willy-nilly,

run,

run,

run.

having fun!

Tumble,
tangle,

Kittens by the pool—
one cat, two.

Don't get wet, cats!

CAT SKIDOO!

Hurry,
scurry,
high and low.

Scritch,
scratch,
scritch,
up cats go!

Kittens in an elm tree—
one cat, two,

jump back down for

CAT SKIDOO!

Helter-skelter
roll and bounce.

Skitter,

scatter,

leap and pounce!

Kittens in the green grass—
one cat, two.

Here comes Dog, so . . .

CAT SKIDOO!

Hide and seek.
Rush,
　　rush,
　　　rush.

Stop! Listen!
Hush,
    hush,
        hush.

Someone's calling—
one cat, two.

Zip,

skip,

CAT SKIDOO.

Scramble up steps,
into the house.

Pit-pat,
   pit-pat,
quiet as a mouse.

Drink that milk—
one cat, two.

Licking,
lapping,
CAT SKIDOO.

yawn and stretch,
and curl up so.

Kittens in a basket—
slower,

slow,

Kittens sleeping—
one cat, two,

purr and dream of
CAT SKIDOO...